WRITTEN BY
DORINE BARBEY AND CHRISTINE LAZIER,
LAURA BOUR, M. CZAJKOWSKI, MARIE FARRÉ, BÉATRICE FONTANEL,
BÉATRICE FONTANEL, DOMINIQUE JOLY, JEAN-PIERRE REYMOND,
CHARLOTTE RUFFAULT, CATHERINE DE SAIRIGNÉ

COVER DESIGN BY
STEPHANIE BLUMENTHAL

TRANSLATED AND ADAPTED BY
LINDA BUTURIAN AND ROSEMARY WALLNER

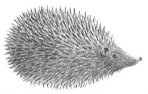

PUBLISHED BY CREATIVE EDUCATION
123 South Broad Street, Mankato, Minnesota 56001
Creative Education is an imprint of The Creative Company

Library of Congress Cataloging-in-Publication Data
[Bétes qui nous entourent. English]
Animals around us / by Dorine Barbey et al. ; [illustrated by Paul Botemps ;
translated and adapted by Linda Buturian].
(Creative Discoveries)
Includes index.
Summary: Describes the behaviors and life cycles of various animals, from dogs, cats, and sheep
to mice, bats, and birds, as well as how they interact with humans.
ISBN: 0-88682-943-7
1. Animals—Juvenile literature.   2. Domestic animals—Juvenile literature.
[1. Animals.   2. Domestic animals.]   I. Barbey, Dorine.   II. Botemps, Paul, ill.   III. Title.   IV Series.
QL49.B557613   1999
590—dc21   First edition   97-27530

2 4 6 8 9 7 5 3 1

ANIMALS AROUND US

CONTENTS

CREATIVE EDUCATION

Lots of insects, spiders, and snails live in our lawns and gardens.

In the country and in the city, many types of tiny animals live around us, sharing our lawns, gardens, and even our homes. Some, like termites and wasps, prefer to stay hidden.

Others, like mosquitoes and flies, are often more visible to us.

All sorts of insects, spiders, and snails live in tall grass. Insects have six legs, a pair of antennae, and often have wings. Spiders have eight legs, but no antennae or wings. At the center of its web, a garden spider waits for its prey. Large silk glands on the spider's body produce silk. Smaller glands, called spinnerets, at the back of the spider's body, spin the silk into thread to make cocoons for their eggs and webs to catch prey. A web may look fragile, but it is strong.

Earwigs are some of the smallest animals around us.

Earwigs, ladybugs, and green June bugs are easy to find in parks and gardens.

Earwigs are insects. They live under stones and in crevices of wood during the day, coming out at night to feed. Because they eat the centers of blossoms, earwigs sometimes turn up in the seeds of fruits like apples or plums. Earwigs look fierce with their big pincers, but they can't hurt people.

Ladybugs are good friends to gardeners. They eat hundreds of those garden pests called aphids—small sluggish insects that suck the juices of plants. A frightened ladybug produces a disgusting smell—enough to put off any hungry bird.

The green June bug is a beetle. June bugs prefer rosebushes. They feed on pollen and fruit. If you touch one, it may pretend to be dead.

When it rains, snails put out their horns. Before winter weather, the female snail lays her eggs in a hole that she digs in the ground. There the eggs stay, protected from the cold and anything that might like to eat them. Then the snail closes over her own shell with a membrane.

By the time snails hatch, they already have a delicate, transparent shell.

Thousands of earthworms reside under every lawn. Earthworms don't simply dig tunnels through the soil—they eat their way through. Since they never stop moving, they eat an enormous amount. Earthworms leave their droppings (little coils of dirt known as "worm casts") on the surface. Earthworms fill the soil with air holes, which let the rain and air soak in.

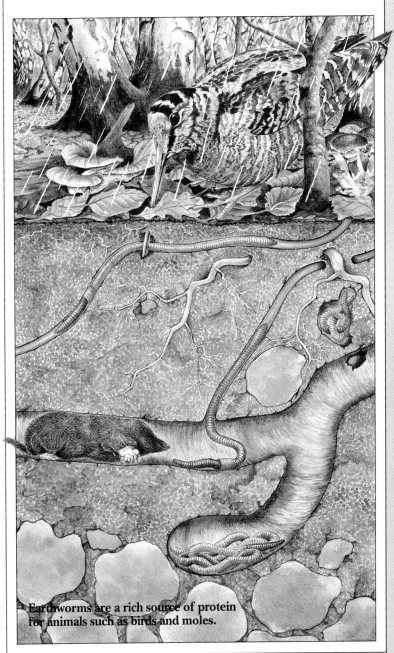

Grasshopper

Earthworms are a rich source of protein for animals such as birds and moles.

We share our homes with many small creatures.

Carpenter ants like the roof and wood frame of buildings. Mosquitoes and flies prefer the rain gutters, and wasps hole up in the chimney. Termites, bees, and other creatures cling to the siding and doors.

Spiders are our friends. They eat all sorts of insects that get trapped in their sticky webs.

Daddy longlegs often escape enemies by leaving a leg behind. Daddy longlegs differ from other spiders because of their long and thin legs and the oval shape of their body.

The most common spider you see in your home is the house spider. It spins its web in

| Housefly | Bluebottle | Greenbottle |

corners, then hides away and waits. When an insect is caught, the spider paralyzes it by injecting poison into the insect's body. Then the spider sucks out the insides of its prey, leaving behind the outer shell.

The creepy-crawly empire of insects
Insects are the most numerous inhabitants of a city—many more flies than people exist. Flies are attracted to leftovers, meat, ripe fruit, and garbage. They settle on food that is left uncovered and lay their eggs. The eggs hatch into maggots, which soon grow into flies.

A cockroach comes out at night, scavenging for scraps of food. The female lays her eggs in an egg case that has tiny, separate compartments for each egg.

Some insects are friends, and others are real pests!

Before they turn into moths, the grubs of clothes moths eat holes in curtains, clothes, and carpets made of natural fibers.

Some insects cause damage to homes. Termites and woodworms eat wood. Their gnawing appetites can reduce a whole roof frame to sawdust. When woodworms emerge, they leave little round holes in the wood. Carpenter ants don't eat wood, but they chew and destroy it faster than termites. These large black ants burrow their nests in damp, rotting wood.

Silverfish have inhabited Earth for more than 350 million years. You can sometimes catch sight of these shy, scaly insects at night, when they come out to find a few crumbs to eat. Occasionally, they chew books because glue and paper are tasty to them too.

Fleas bite and suck our blood, but they can live for several months without eating. Cat fleas are so tiny you can hardly see them, but they can jump almost a foot (30 cm) high— an amazing feat for their size.

Woodlouse

Woodworm

A woodlouse is not an insect; it's a crustacean. They can be found in dark, damp places like basements and under rocks and decaying wood. They roll into a ball and play dead when they are threatened.

Silverfish

Crane flies flutter into homes during the winter months, looking for warmth and light. These long, slender creatures look like giant mosquitoes, but they are harmless and gentle. In the spring, they need to escape from inside out into the sunlight. Many exhaust themselves as they flutter against the windowpanes. If you see them, open the window and let them out.

Bees, ants, and termites live in colonies.

Bees buzzing from flower to flower, ants marching single file to feast on sugar, termites burrowing in their castles of clay—all these insects live in social groups. They can't survive on their own. These groups are like little countries, with a queen, soldiers, and workers. The members of the same group recognize each other by scent.

Beekeepers check their beehives.

Termites are white and blind, and they eat wood. Termites rarely leave their nests because air dries their bodies and could kill them. They prefer warm, humid climates. They live in house timbers and dead trees. They damage homes severely by chewing and digging tunnels through the wood to make their nests. In nature, termites help to convert plants into pulp that can be recycled in the ecosystem to support new life.

In countries with hot climates, termites use mud and their saliva to build huge towers, sometimes as high as 20 feet (6 m)! Inside, the nest is a maze of tunnels leading to storerooms with twigs, leaves, and bits of old wood. There are also secret rooms to hide from attackers. In the middle of the colony lies the enormous, swollen queen. Unable to move, she simply lays egg after egg. The king and a band of workers wait on her.

Termites talk to each other by tapping, like Morse code. When danger threatens, they tap on the wood. The warning sends everyone hurrying for safety in the heart of the nest.

1. Queen 2. Workers 3. King 4. Soldiers

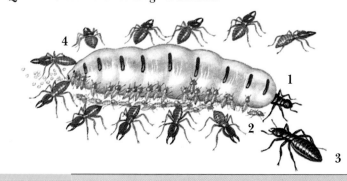

Bees have many different jobs.

Bees can walk upside down on the ceiling using the tiny claws on their feet.

A beehive has 50,000 inhabitants; that's as many as a small city. Nearly all the bees are female worker bees. They take turns being nurses, builders, housekeepers, food carriers, and soldiers. In most countries bees are kept to make the honey we eat. In the United States more than 200,000 beekeepers keep domestic bees in small wooden beehives. Wild bees live in hollow tree trunks.

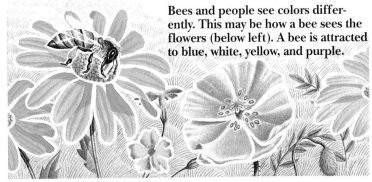

Bees and people see colors differently. This may be how a bee sees the flowers (below left). A bee is attracted to blue, white, yellow, and purple.

Bees and flowers have a wonderful relationship! Bees pollinate flowers by carrying pollen from one flower to another flower of the same kind. While the plant uses some of the pollen to produce its fruits and seeds, the bee carries the rest of the pollen and the sweet liquid nectar back to the hive. Pollen is for feeding larvae; the nectar is used to make honey. Inside the hive, the bees produce wax in tiny flakes from glands on their abdomen. They chew the wax to soften it, then shape it into cells.

Worker   Male, or drone   Queen

The queen is the mother of all the bees. Fertilized by male bees called drones, the queen lays thousands of eggs, day and night. The eggs are placed in tiny wax cells. After three days, the larvae hatch. Worker bees, acting as nurses, feed them a mixture of pollen and honey.

Still damp, this newborn bee has just come out of its cell.

Ants are extremely smart, social animals.

Life in an ants' nest is organized. Like bees, ants have a queen, workers, and soldiers. But some ants live longer than bees—the workers live for about a year, and the queen can live up to 12 years.

How is an ants' nest built? In midsummer, the young queens fly away. Each finds a hole, sheds her wings, and crawls inside to lay her eggs. A few weeks later, the larvae hatch into ants. Soon they are busy making the nest bigger, using twigs, saliva, and moss. Ants can lift about 50 times their own body weight.

They dig special rooms to store their food and protect their young. The eggs, larvae, and cocoons each have their own chamber. Ants even make doors that they can shut at night.

Worker   Male   Queen

Ants are helpful to the environment.

Ants play a crucial role in nature. They help to control the population of their prey, recycle plant matter, disperse seeds, and turn the soil. As ants churn up the soil, air is able to reach the roots of plants.

The young queen ants fly off to start new colonies.

Ants have huge appetites. They eat seeds, leaves, fruit, and other insects. A large colony of ants will consume as many as 10,000 insects a day. Some ants love the sweet honeydew they can get from aphids. They stroke them with their antennae, "milking" them of the substance. The aphid lifts its rear end and a tiny droplet appears, which the ant quickly drinks. Ants often take aphids into their nests to protect them from insects like ladybugs and to provide themselves with a dependable food source. Ants are attracted to sweets and will march by the thousands into homes to devour a drop of jam or honey.

A small pile of twigs in the woods might be the roof of an ants' nest.

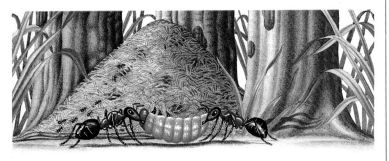

Ants feast on a grasshopper.

Ants communicate through scents. When an ant finds prey that is too big to carry, it calls its friends by leaving small drops of scent along its trail—a signal to other ants that says "come and help." Ants have a whole language of smells: one special smell means "Danger!" and another means "Feed the queen."

Honey ants

Weaver ants from Asia work as a team.
They make a nest out of leaves, which they sew together with a silky thread produced by their grubs. If the leaves grow too far apart, the ants form a chain to pull them together.

If you could weigh all the ants on Earth, they would weigh more than all of the other creatures combined! Ants are everywhere.

Perhaps you have only seen the large black

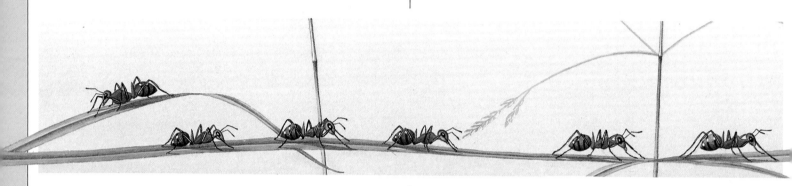

ants and the small reddish-brown ants common in the United States. But more than 6,000 other kinds of ants exist. Honey ants make their home in the southwestern United States. The worker ants gather honeydew in a special pouch near their stomach called a crop. When they return to the nest, they spit food into the mouths of other ants that hang upside down and share their honey when food is scarce.

Sword-like mandibles help slave-making ants capture workers. Some ants can't use their jaws for food or tending their young. Instead they use them for fighting. They raid the nests of smaller black ants and carry their pupa back to their own nests. The young black ants become their slaves.

Ants have different defense mechanisms.
Some ants bite, and some ants squirt poisonous acid to defend themselves. Others sting, like the pesky fire ants of the Southwest. Fire ants build nests as large as three feet (90 cm) across. They sting humans, livestock, pets, and wildlife.

Weaver ants

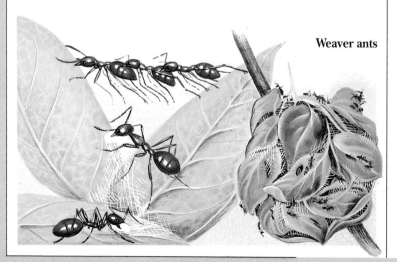

African army ants are fierce.

The terrible African army ants are aggressive and hungry. They walk long distances, marching at about 115 feet (35 m) per hour in columns made up of thousands of ants.

Swarms of African army ants attack and eat anything that gets in their way. The ants in this picture are just starting to eat a snake.

If a larger animal, or even a person, gets in their way, they swarm all over the body. Their bites are very painful.

Leaf-cutter ants from South America swarm up trees by the thousands to cut down leaves with their steely sharp jaws. They carry the leaves back to their nests, where they make a sort of compost to grow the fungus that they eat.

Leaf-cutter ants

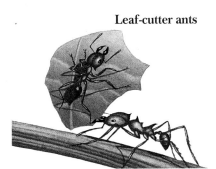

From caterpillar to butterfly or moth

On hot days in parks and gardens, you can see butterflies fluttering from flower to flower, sucking nectar. Their wings are covered with thousands of tiny scales, arranged in beautiful patterns. More than 100,000 different kinds of butterflies and moths exist. Like bees, butterflies and moths help to pollinate flowers and enable them to grow.

The wings of a male and female Emperor Moth have different patterns.

A butterfly or moth passes through four stages of life: egg, caterpillar, chrysalis, and adult. Many butterflies and moths spend most of their lives as caterpillars. Most caterpillars live in groups; a butterfly or moth usually lives on its own. For a long time, people thought caterpillars and butterflies were two completely different animals.

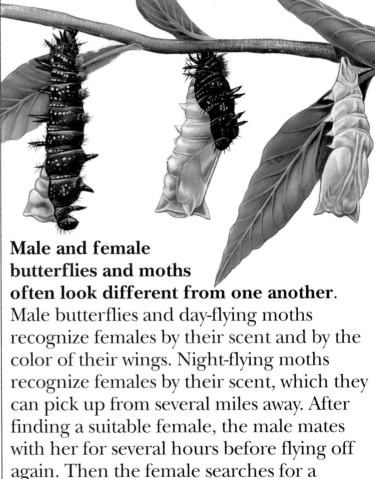

Male and female butterflies and moths often look different from one another. Male butterflies and day-flying moths recognize females by their scent and by the color of their wings. Night-flying moths recognize females by their scent, which they can pick up from several miles away. After finding a suitable female, the male mates with her for several hours before flying off again. Then the female searches for a desirable place to lay her eggs.

What an amazing change!

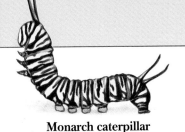
Monarch caterpillar

Morpho caterpillar

Charaxes caterpillar

Garden Tiger Moth caterpillar

Some female butterflies lay 25 eggs, some as many as several thousand. Many lay their eggs on plants that they recognize by smell. Then they know the newly hatched caterpillars will have plenty to eat. When the caterpillar is ready to hatch, it chews a hole in the shell with its tiny jaws and wriggles out of the egg. It eats the rest of the eggshell, and then begins eating the plant. Before long, it has grown very fat and its skin becomes too tight. It's time for a new one.

When the change from pupa to butterfly is complete, it splits open the chrysalis and pulls itself free. First, the butterfly contracts its muscles so that blood can begin to circulate through the veins in its wings. Gradually, the limp, damp wings spread and dry, and the butterfly is ready to fly.

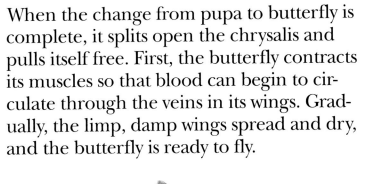

A White Admiral butterfly emerges from its chrysalis.

This is called molting. Most caterpillars shed their skins about five times. When the caterpillar is ready to become a butterfly, it changes color and its skin becomes thinner. Next, it forms a hard shell, called a chrysalis, around itself. It doesn't eat or move until the butterfly is formed. This can take anywhere from eight days to four years, depending on the species and the climate.

Most caterpillars feed on plants.

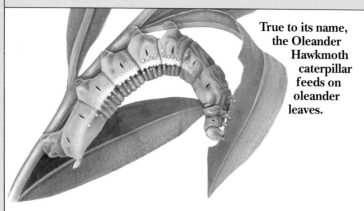

True to its name, the Oleander Hawkmoth caterpillar feeds on oleander leaves.

leaves. Many caterpillars eat only one sort of plant all their life.

A few caterpillars live in tree trunks or in the horns or hooves of animals. There isn't much to eat, so those caterpillars grow slowly. Some caterpillars live underwater. They wrap themselves in a silky, waterproof blanket under a water lily leaf and breathe the oxygen the plant releases.

Caterpillars have suckers and small hooks on their stubby legs that help them hang onto

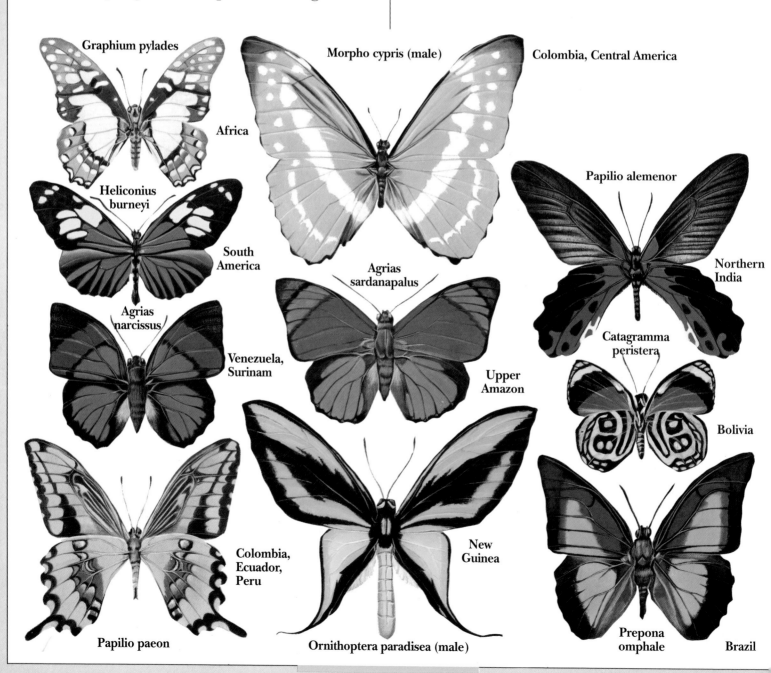

Graphium pylades

Africa

Heliconius burneyi

South America

Agrias narcissus

Venezuela, Surinam

Morpho cypris (male)

Colombia, Central America

Agrias sardanapalus

Upper Amazon

Papilio alemenor

Northern India

Catagramma peristera

Bolivia

Papilio paeon

Colombia, Ecuador, Peru

Ornithoptera paradisea (male)

New Guinea

Prepona omphale

Brazil

Butterflies and moths drink nectar from flowers.

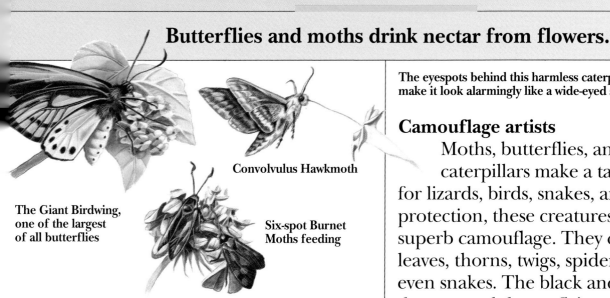

Convolvulus Hawkmoth

The Giant Birdwing, one of the largest of all butterflies

Six-spot Burnet Moths feeding

Flowers secrete a sweet liquid called nectar. Most butterflies and moths suck up nectar through a tube called a proboscis. The length of the proboscis varies according to the depth of the flowers on which the butterfly usually feeds.

Butterflies and moths use their antennae as scent organs, which are far more sensitive than human noses. The slightest trace of scent is enough to guide them to a certain flower. Also, a monarch's sensitivity to taste is more than 2,000 times greater than a human's tongue. Most butterflies and moths only live for a month or two, though those

Painted Lady   Red Admiral   Small Tortoiseshell

that hibernate may survive up to nine months. Species that do not have a proboscis don't feed, and their lives are very short.

When the Eyed Hawkmoth opens its wings suddenly, the action is enough to scare off this thrush.

The eyespots behind this harmless caterpillar's head make it look alarmingly like a wide-eyed snake.

Camouflage artists

Moths, butterflies, and caterpillars make a tasty meal for lizards, birds, snakes, and monkeys. As protection, these creatures have developed superb camouflage. They can look like leaves, thorns, twigs, spiders, hornets, and even snakes. The black and yellow stripes on the monarch butterfly's caterpillar warns birds that it's poisonous.

Parks and gardens are the wildlife reserves of cities.

In the spring, parks and gardens burst with activity. At dawn, many different species of birds start to sing, marking out their territory and attracting mates. Birds live both in rural and urban settings; many species have adapted to city life because of the abundance of food there. Garbage cans, bird feeders, and flower beds provide good things to eat all year round.

House sparrows twitter at the pavement's edge.

The sparrow is a chatty bird. While it builds its nest, the sparrow sometimes repeats its song 300 times in an hour.

Birds may travel hundreds of miles as they fly back and forth with food for their young.

Warblers are one of nature's acrobats. Have you ever seen them doing their tricks on the very tip of a branch, as they try to catch an insect?

The goldfinch is easy to recognize with its bright yellow body and black-and-white wings. It is fond of eating thistle and sunflower seeds.

When milk was delivered to homes, birds often pecked through the cap to drink the cream.

1. Grosbeak
2. European Goldfinch
3. Chickadee
4. Nuthatch
5. Flycatcher
6. Cat
7. Blackbird
8. Magpie

Twigs, moss, feathers, and grass are useful for building a nest.

Birds place their nests on the ground, in bushes, or high up in trees and buildings. Birds choose a nesting site carefully. The nest needs to be hidden from predators and sheltered from the wind and rain, so the chicks will be protected.

Blackbirds build their nests in a bush or in hedges.

What's good for making a nest?

The chick breaks out of its shell using its egg tooth, a hard little tooth at the end of its beak.

Spider's webs, feathers, and fluff make the inside soft and cozy. Twigs, leaves, and moss are good for the walls. It takes at least a week, and sometimes two or three, before the nest is finished. Some nests are the size of a thimble, others are as big as a tractor tire!

Who sits on the eggs? Sometimes just the female bird, or just the male, but usually

both take turns. Most birds incubate their eggs as soon as they have been laid. Then the eggs will all hatch at the same time. The parents have to leave the nest regularly to find something to eat.

The chicks hatch. Under the repeated tapping of the chick inside, the shell gives way at last. It can take hours for the chick to break out of its shell. Baby birds in a nest have to be fed nonstop from dawn to dusk. The bright orange of their gaping beaks attracts the parents, who pop in a beakful of food. Sometimes the food has been partly digested into a pulp.

If their young are too tired to swim, adult swans and grebes carry them on their back.

Soon they are ready to fly!

Robin   Grouse   Killdeer

With or without feathers

Some chicks hatch covered in down and can follow their parents out of the nest right away. Ducklings take to the water, and baby killdeer totter along on spindly legs. Other chicks, like robins, are born blind and without feathers, and they stay in the nest. Their parents look after them until they are ready to fly.

The first flight

As the chicks grow, they become plump and well-fed and their feathers develop. They practice

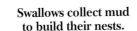

Swallows collect mud to build their nests.

beating their wings and tumble out of the nest, one after the other. The babies aren't very good fliers at first, and their parents keep an eye on them for the next few days until they can fly safely.

A coot gets up the speed for takeoff by running on the water. On the bank, the mallard drake keeps watch while his less brightly colored mate rests in the cattails.

You can see many birds from the edge of a pond or a riverbank. You might see a Red-necked grebe preening its feathers to keep them clean and waterproof. Or you might spot the shy, little grebe hiding among the reeds. It dives into the water again and again, looking for fish to catch.

Moorhens pick their way along the bank. Dippers fish from the shallows. If you're really lucky, you might see the brilliant flash of blue as a kingfisher dives.

Buildings and trees provide ready-made shelter for birds.

In Europe, storks nest on top of chimneys. In the southeastern part of the United States, the wood stork lives in colonies high up in trees near marshes, lakes, and lagoons. Barn owls sleep all day in attics, barns, and shade trees. At night, they patrol the edges of fields for mice and moles.

Caw! Caw! That's a crow's harsh cry from its perch up on the rooftops. Crows are often found near people.

Kestrels are small hawks. They sometimes build their nests in old buildings, on the tops of skyscrapers, and in hollow trees. They pump their tails as they keep a lookout from telephone wires. Kestrels and barn owls are both birds of prey, meaning they hunt live food, but kestrels hunt by day rather than by night.

Look up and see what kinds of birds are on the rooftops.

Is there a nest on your home? House martins use mud and twigs to build their nests under the eaves of houses. They come back to the same nest every year. Pigeons seem to rule the roost in cities. They swagger along the pavements, hardly bothering to get out of your way.

They build their nests on the ledges of tall buildings, which remind them of the cliffs where their ancestors used to live.

Chimney swifts fly about 100 miles (175 km) per hour. They roost clinging to chimneys and spend most of their time in the air. They can catch insects as they fly. At night, they rest by gliding high up in the sky.

Up above the rivers and canals, gulls hover and turn. At night they leave the city to sleep by a marsh or nearby pond.

After 28 days, ducklings hatch and waddle down behind their mother for their first swim.

Geese and ducks secrete a sort of wax that coats their feathers to keep them waterproof.

Chickens, ducks, geese, and turkeys all originally came from the wild. You can still find wild turkeys in the forests and countryside across the United States. Farm animals have been living under the care of people for thousands of years. Chickens were the first domestic animal. Today, huge poultry farms keep several thousand laying hens. A hen can produce as many as 200 eggs a year.

In the United States, most geese are still kept in small farm flocks. Goose feathers are used to make down pillows, coats, and sleeping bags.

Ducks dive head first into the water to search for worms, waterweeds, and tadpoles to eat. A duck's webbed feet help it to swim.

In Africa, guinea fowl live in groups and have a pecking order. They often fight.

Turkeys are the largest farm birds. They can weigh up to 45 pounds (20 kg).

Some birds are kept as pets in cages.

Zebra finches

Yellow-crested cockatoos love eating the seeds of melons, pumpkins, and apples.

Parakeets

Canaries

This gray parrot from Gabon in West Africa can sing, as well as talk.

Birds make graceful pets. Parakeets need a large cage or an aviary to show off their acrobatic skills. Their strong beaks are made for cracking open hard seed pods. They don't have any teeth, so they eat grit to grind the food they have swallowed.

Parakeets are the most popular caged bird in the United States. They are inexpensive and can be trained to sit on your finger and eat from your hand.

How do parrots and cockatoos talk? A special organ at the base of their throat allows them to mimic the human voice.

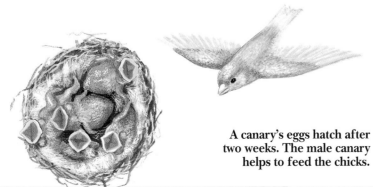

Lovebirds

Lovebirds from Africa and Madagascar deserve their name—they spend a lot of time huddling together, and they mate for life, something few other birds do.

In India, China, Malaysia, and Japan, people have bred mynah birds for thousands of years. In captivity, mynah birds can imitate the human voice. They pick up phrases and learn tunes, repeating them without any mistakes. The best talkers among the American parrots are the Amazons. They are some of the longest-living birds in the world. Many captive Amazons have even out-lived their owners!

Mynah bird

If you keep birds in a cage, give them somewhere to perch, a swing, separate bowls for food and water, and a birdbath.

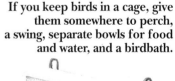

A canary's eggs hatch after two weeks. The male canary helps to feed the chicks.

Canaries like to eat birdseed, lettuce, dried cuttlefish bone, and millet.

Strong little gnawing teeth nibble at everything.

Gardens, and sometimes houses too, are home to many small rodents. Some are not welcome! In the 18th century, the house rat came to the United States by boat from Asia. Rats live in basements, sewers, and garbage dumpsters and eat over a million tons of human food a year. They are very intelligent and hard to catch.

Rats are wonderful acrobats.

A hamster washes itself—it rubs its front paws over its ears and eyes, and then licks its fingers.

Brown rats live in groups and hunt for food at night. They run along the edge of walls and squeak in their shrill voices. They are great swimmers. They also go into all sorts of dirty places and transmit diseases.

Mice live everywhere. They make nests under floorboards or in a hole in the wall, out of bits of paper that they have taken from us. Mice may not eat much, but they'll eat anything!

Do you own a pet hamster? These animals stuff food into their cheek pouches and then empty it into a corner for later. Hamsters live wild in southern Europe.

Rabbits live happily outdoors in a hutch. Rabbits like eating hay, alfalfa, lettuce, fruit, dried bread, and pellets. They need something to gnaw on so their teeth don't grow too long. A rabbit should never be held by its ears; support its body.

Moles hoard earthworms; bats eat thousands of insects nightly.

Moles are tireless diggers. They tunnel underground, using their front paws that are shaped like shovels.

A mole's fur stands straight up, so it won't get rubbed the wrong way if the mole has to go backward down a tunnel.

A tunneling mole pushes the dirt aside, slicing through roots with its sharp claws. Its back packs the dirt hard against the walls. Moles are almost blind. They have 12 whiskers on their muzzle and others on their paws and tail. The whiskers tell them when something is in their way. Moles dig to find the worms they eat. They bite the worms, then hoard them, unconscious but still alive, in underground chambers.

Hedgehogs are a close relative to the mole. Found in Europe, Asia, and Africa, hedgehogs have a coat of long stiff spines on their backs. Hedgehogs spend the day fast asleep, rolled up in a ball. At night, they snuffle and snort around the garden looking for mollusks, worms, and insects to eat.

Hanging upside down, wrapped in leathery wings, a bat waits for nightfall so it can hunt.

Bats are the only mammals that can truly fly. Furry, with a fox-like face, they have feet and wings as well. Bats sleep all day, hanging upside down in attics, barns, and caves, coming out at night to hunt. Bats have small eyes, and they rely on their ears to find their way around. They send out pulses of ultrasound, too high for humans to hear. Their highly sensitive ears pick up the echo as the sounds bounce off objects around them. Even in pitch darkness, they never bump into anything. Bats eat moths, flies, and many other insects, and can send out their ultrasonic squeaks

even with their mouths full. They drink by skimming the surface of ponds without slowing their flight. Sometimes they lick dew off plants. There are 40 different species of bats in the U.S.

A bat's large ears help it pick up vibrations of ultrasound.

Watch a cat—you could be looking at a miniature tiger!

The cat is a domestic animal, a familiar pet, and a dear friend. Listen to it purring with pleasure as you stroke its fur. But watch for a moment as it slinks on silent paws around the house or springs to the top of the sofa in a single bound. Its supple, graceful movements are like its wild cousins, the African lion, the Asian tiger, and the puma of the Rocky Mountains.

The cat and its cousins are mammals and members of the large family of felines. All felines are carnivorous, which means they like eating meat. A cat's pointed canine teeth are sharp daggers that are used for killing birds and mice. Further back, the molar teeth grind the meat into pieces small enough to swallow.

Angora

Turkish

Maine Coon

Persian

Bobtail

Scottish Fold

Egyptian Mau

Silver Tabby

Peke-faced Persian

Himalayan

Birman

Cream Short-hair

Burmese

Russian Blue

Foreign Lilac

Manx

Balinese

Abyssinian

Somali

Siamese

Oriental

Bombay

American Wirehair

Cymric

Chartreux

Ocicat

Rex

Sphinx

A cat has highly developed senses of smell, sight, and hearing.

A cat stalks a mouse noiselessly. It stops, then springs with a single bound, and grabs its prey between sharp claws.

Cats only unsheathe their claws when they need to grip something.

The cat is a hunter, like all felines, with strong muscles and sharp eyes. All cats can see in the dark. Their pupils open wide, and special reflectors at the back of their eyes double the light available. Their claws can be drawn back inside their toes to help keep them needle-sharp.

Cats use their whiskers to measure the width of gaps that they crawl through. In dim light, a cat uses its whiskers to feel its way along.

A cat sleeps a lot during the day.

Watch a cat jump! It leaps like an uncoiled spring.

Cats walk on the pads of their toes—a movement called digitigrade. Cats are very good at balancing. They can prowl around on narrow walls and rooftops without falling off.

Cats use their rough, sandpaper-like tongues to lick their fur from head to toe. They lift out dead hair and dust, and use their teeth to pull off any dirt that is sticking to their fur. Saliva also helps to make a cat feel clean.

Cats twist and bend to lick and nibble at every part of their bodies.

Sometimes it "cat naps" with one eye open. At other times, it falls into a deep sleep.

If a cat falls, it can turn in the air and still land on its feet.

Ginger cat

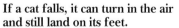

Are you as flexible as a cat?

Kittens love to play.

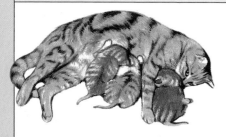

A female cat can have up to six kittens in a litter. The kittens are blind, deaf, and almost hairless at birth. Their mother feeds them for about eight weeks.

Kittens are fun! They are lively, full of mischief, and love to play. Kittens often purr when they are content or while they sleep.

There's a reason for all these games of catch and pounce: the kitten is learning to use its muscles, teeth, and claws.

Time for a snooze! When a kitten wakes up, it yawns and stretches from its claws to its tail—then suddenly it's off again! You never know what a kitten is going to do next. If you scold a cat, it may sit down and lick its shoulder, sulking. A young lion reacts in just the same way when it is put in its place by an older one.

Cats as pets

Before cats lived with people, the genet, a cat-like cousin of the mongoose, was the mouser around the house.

Dogs were the first domestic animals trained for hunting. Then people started to rear cows, sheep, and pigs. Other animals, like the horse, elephant, and camel, were trained to carry people on their backs or help with fieldwork.

The last animal to be domesticated was the cat. Cats learned to live in partnership with people, catching rats and mice in return for food and warmth. But even today, they keep their independent streak—many cats can look after themselves.

A wildcat: many small wildcats lead a hidden, secret life away from people.

Wolves once roamed in great numbers throughout the United States.

You may have seen a wolf in the zoo, pacing up and down in its cage, but have you seen one in the wild? Where are they? When the settlers first came to North America, wolves roamed the prairies, forests, and mountains. Hunting and development of the land have greatly reduced their numbers. The largest population of gray wolves is in Alaska. Some wolves live scattered throughout the western and midwestern states as well.

The red wolf still roams the south central United States.

Little Red Riding Hood

Worldwide, large populations live in parts of Europe and Asia, but in countries such as Great Britain, the wolf has become extinct.

The wolf's greatest enemies are human beings. For hundreds of years, people thought that wolves were ferocious monsters. They did not understand how wolves lived, and made up frightening stories about how wolves devoured humans. Remember Little Red Riding Hood and the Big, Bad Wolf?

Few healthy wolves have attacked humans. Wolves try to avoid people whenever possible, and for good reason.

Mothers once scolded their children by telling them stories of a Big Bad Wolf that would come and get them if they were naughty. Those stories have given wolves a false image as killers.

People always have hunted wolves.

Before they had guns, villagers used to hunt wolves with sturdy dogs and strong sticks.

A wolf hunt: people needed teams of dogs to keep up with the fast-running wolves.

Kill the wolf! All through the centuries, farmers and hunters have thought of wolves as enemies because they kill livestock and wildlife. People have killed wolves in many ways: traps, dogs, guns, and poison.

How did people keep wolves away? When the biting north wind drove hungry wolves toward a village, a "wolf tile" on the ridge of a house roof acted as a warning signal. The wind whistled through the holes in the tile, warning villagers that wolves might be prowling around.

Guard dogs wore spiked collars to protect their throats from a wolf's jaws. Herbs like wolfsbane were supposed to keep wolves away. Lights, fires, and loud noises worked better to scare off the wolves.

The last wild wolf in France was killed in 1977.

The wolf has a necessary place in nature. Wolves help to control the number of grazing animals as well as weak and wounded animals. Wolves are a part of nature's balance, where only the strong survive and breed. In some places where wolves have disappeared, other predators, like foxes, have taken their place.

Bringing back the wolf

In the United States, efforts are being made to reintroduce wolves to a few national parks. Recently, gray wolves were set free in Yellowstone National Park, and red wolves were released in the Great Smoky Mountain National Park.

Wolf light

Whirling this rope made the carved shape screech.

No wolf would attack a dog with spikes like this on its neck.

Hunting wolves from helicopters meant simple slaughter. This kind of massacre is forbidden now.

A dominant male and female wolf mate for life.

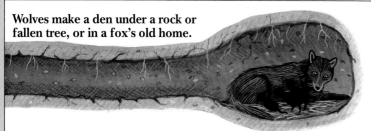

Wolves make a den under a rock or fallen tree, or in a fox's old home.

Only the pack's dominant male and female mate. In spring, they look for a quiet spot where they can raise their young. After nine weeks, the female gives birth to as many as seven jet-black cubs, which she nurses.

As soon as they can walk, the wolf cubs set off to explore.

Wolves have an extremely varied diet. Wolves eat large animals such as deer, moose, and elk. But they also eat all kinds of smaller animals, such as beavers, rabbits, and frogs. When food is scarce, wolves are not choosy: they will eat snakes, worms, and even berries. Trotting upstream, wolves push salmon into shallow pools and catch them with one snap of their powerful jaws. A wolf never kills for pleasure, only for food.

All the wolves in the pack chew up meat to feed the cubs.

In winter, wolves group together in packs.

Wolves use the pack system to hunt large animals. So as not to waste energy, wolves test large prey before they attack by following about 100 yards (100 m) behind it. If it is fast and fit, they leave it alone and choose an older and weaker animal.

Once they have chased down their prey, wolves surround it and draw closer together. At last the animal is brought to bay. The wolves leap and kill the prey quickly with their sharp fangs.

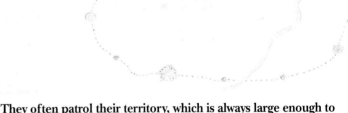

Wolves, like dogs, mark the limits of their territory with a few drops of urine on landmarks such as stones and bushes.

They often patrol their territory, which is always large enough to supply all their food and encloses a stream.

In winter, a pack of five to eight wolves groups together under the leadership of a dominant wolf and his female.

They are the two strongest wolves. Only this couple will breed, though all the others in the pack will hunt together to feed the cubs.

Wolves walk in single file, nose to tail, through the snow, leaving only one set of prints.

But when they go around curves, they fan out, and you can tell how many wolves are in the pack.

Both wild and domestic dogs are cousins of the wolf.

Cape hunting dogs live in packs of up to 30 animals.

Dingoes live and hunt in small packs.

On the outskirts of big cities, coyotes love rummaging about in garbage cans.

Which animals are related to wolves? Cape hunting dogs, or painted hyenas, live on the plains of Africa. They take great care of their young. When the pack has killed, the pups take the first turn at feeding.

Jackals don't only scavenge for dead meat—they are good hunters too.

Dingoes, the wild dogs of Australia, arrived on that continent about 6,000 years ago. They look a lot like the earliest dogs we know about.

Prairie wolves, or coyotes, live in North America. They like eating fruit just as much as they like eating rabbits and fawns. Coyotes can run at speeds up to 40 miles (64 km) per hour. They can be heard at night yapping and howling at each other.

Jackals are small, smoother-coated animals. They live on the plains of Africa and eastern Europe. They hunt at night in family groups.

Some dogs look like their wild ancestors. The German shepherd dog, or Alsatian, is often said to look like a wolf. These dogs make good guard dogs, and also help mountain rescue teams.

Can you see the differences between an Alsatian and a wolf?

Half dog, half wolf

Some Inuit tribes use powerful dogs to pull their sleds. The Innuit sometimes allow a wild, male wolf to mate with one of their females. The young combine the size and endurance of wolves with the loyalty of dogs. These animals are fierce and have to be trained well.

German shepherd

One dog from Africa, called a Basenji, can't bark.

There are about 400 different breeds of dogs.

The origins of domestic dogs are still unknown. They may have descended from jackals or Asian wild dogs, but their ancestors were probably wolves.

The ancient Egyptians loved dogs and thought they were sacred. Anyone who harmed a dog was punished. When a pet dog died, it was made into a mummy and often buried in the family tomb.

These dachshunds sniff one another to get to know each other.

Dogs come in different shapes and sizes. A Chihuahua is only as tall as three apples stacked on top of one another. An Irish wolfhound can grow to three feet (90 cm) tall. Some dogs have long bodies, like basset hounds; some have smashed noses, like bulldogs; and others have long, slim legs like greyhounds.

Pomeranian

Irish wolfhound

Bulldog

Wire-haired fox terrier

Brittany spaniel

Shar Pei

A dog can be a faithful friend.

Excited   Relaxed   Scared   Happy

Tail-language tells you how a dog is feeling.

Dogs are loyal and affectionate companions. Often they are more than just pets; they become part of the family.

Dogs that are well-cared for will be obedient. A dog will obey you if you train it properly. It should learn to walk and heel on a leash. Be firm with your dog, but never hit it. Praise and pet your dog when it does what it's told. You will be able to tell how it's feeling from the way it looks, especially from the position of its tail. Let a new puppy run around inside the house. It will explore its new territory by sniffing around. It may start to whimper because it misses its mother, brothers, and sisters. Cuddle and play with it.

Puppies love to chew. In order for their permanent teeth to come in properly, puppies need to chew. Give your puppy toys it can chew, like a meat-scented nylon bone. Otherwise it will use your shoes or furniture.

A fully grown male dog lifts his leg when he urinates, marking out his territory by leaving a few drops of urine.

A dog's paws have pads underneath, so you could say they are walking on their fingertips. They cannot retract their claws like cats can.

A dog's dinner
Dog food should contain meat protein. Some people add vegetables, oil, eggs, meat, or vitamins to their dog's meal. Dog biscuits clean and strengthen your dog's teeth.

They may be enemies in the wild, but these five animals are obviously good friends!

A litter of puppies

Puppies like to sniff all over the place.

Two months after mating, a female gives birth to her puppies. Between four and 10 young are in a litter. Newborn puppies cannot see or hear, but they know their mother's smell. She has to eat three times as much as normal to produce enough milk to feed them. A dog's milk is much richer than cows' milk, and the puppies double their weight in a week. Just like children, puppies lose their milk, or "baby," teeth. They grow adult teeth by the time they're seven months old.

The ticking of the clock reminds this lonely puppy of his mother's heartbeat and helps him go to sleep.

King Charles Spaniels

Boars are the wild pigs of the forests and mountains.

Long ago, all pigs were wild. In the United States there are still two kinds of wild pigs: peccaries and boars.

Peccaries are native to North America. They live on the East and West coasts and in the Southwest desert. Peccaries are smaller than farm pigs and have tusks.

Wild boars came from Europe. The British brought them to North America for sport hunting. They stand three feet (90 cm) high and weigh up to 400 pounds (181 kg). They feed on seeds, roots, insects, and small animals. During the day, they rest in their lairs, dug deep in the undergrowth.

Boars have tough skin and thick bristles. The female, or sow, makes a bed of leaves and moss for her piglets.

Until they are about six months old, the piglets have striped coats that keep them hidden in the dappled light of the forest. At about five years old, the young males leave the family group and live alone. Wild boars are the last large wild animal in Europe.

A boar's color changes as it grows older. In old age, its coat turns a grizzled gray.

In the Middle Ages, domestic pigs looked very different.

What were pigs like in the Middle Ages?
They were half like their ancestors, the wild boars, and half like the pigs of today. They lived in people's homes and walked freely about the streets.

A swineherd would take the pigs out into the forests to find food. The animals ate berries, mushrooms, birds' eggs, acorns, hazelnuts, chestnuts, and beech nuts. The swineherd let the pigs wander and called them back in the evening.

Today, pigs are kept in pigsties or fields.
The farmer feeds them cereals and root vegetables that are tipped into their feeding troughs. Out in the fields, pigs grub up roots, grass, and insects as well. Pigs are omnivorous, meaning they eat most things.

Pigs are not dirty! Have you heard the phrase "dirty as a pig"? Pigs are actually clean animals. They roll in the mud to get cool and remove any blood-sucking insects that make them itch. Pigs grunt with pleasure as they enjoy their mud baths.

Pigs are naturally friendly. When they are kept in tiny pens with hardly any room to move about, they become unhappy and aggressive. Sometimes they bite each other. With more space, pigs get more exercise and do not get as fat. They are also calmer and much happier.

Pigs are mischievous and intelligent animals. They can learn to open a gate, lifting the latch with their snout.

A pig is a great character, a favorite on the farm.

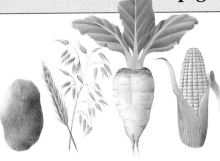

On a pig's menu are potatoes, cereals, turnips, and corn.

Pigs are heavy. A fully grown pig is about 10 times heavier than most children. It has a thick layer of fat under its skin and a coat of stiff hair, or bristles. Pigs have four toes on each pointed trotter, or foot, but they only stand on the front two toes.

A male is called a boar, and a female is a sow (just like those in the wild). A sow gives birth to between six and 20 piglets in a litter, and she produces two litters a year. Each piglet weighs more than two pounds (1 kg) at birth, but six months later they will be almost 100 times that weight. A sow has 12 nipples, and each piglet has its own one.

Piglets have sharp canine teeth that the farmer clips to stop them from hurting each other. Pigs live for about seven years, if they are not killed earlier for meat.

One in three pigs lives in China.

The Chinese people first started to raise pigs thousands of years ago. Now, one in three of all pigs in the world live in China. The 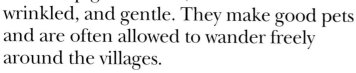 Chinese pigs are black, wrinkled, and gentle. They make good pets and are often allowed to wander freely around the villages.

In many Mediterranean countries, pigs are allowed to roam free also. They live and forage in the forests, especially wherever there are oak trees growing. They provide acorns on which the pigs feed.

In the United States, most pigs are raised in "factory-farm" feedlots where thousands of the animals are kept in tiny cages inside clean, air-conditioned barns.

In Africa, pigs wander wherever they want around the houses. They find their own food, keeping an eye open for kitchen scraps, plants, and roots.

Taking a pig for a walk on a leash

It's a hard life as there is not much food to spare. But the pigs manage, growing long and lean because they haven't been specially bred to be heavy and fat.

In Thailand, the Akha people rear pigs in their villages, up in the mountain forests.

Would you like a pig for a pet? In the United States, the miniature potbellied pig has become a popular pet. The animals are usually about a foot high (30 cm) and weigh close to 40 pounds (18 kg). People take them out for walks as if they were dogs. Potbellied pigs sometimes live to be 12 years old, and they are intelligent.

In Papua New Guinea, the more pigs a family has, the richer it is. Baby pigs are treated almost like one of the family, living in the house, eating nice meals, being taken for walks on a leash. When the pig is fully grown, it is eaten at a big feast. Inviting many people to come and eat your pig is one way of showing how rich you are.

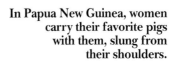

In Papua New Guinea, women carry their favorite pigs with them, slung from their shoulders.

Goats are close relatives of sheep.

Out in the country, a flock of sheep grazing in a field is a common sight. Sheep are hardy animals and stay outside all winter. Goats do well in dry areas. Both are bred for their wool, meat, and milk.

The ancestor of today's domestic sheep is the wild mountain sheep, or mouflon. More than 10,000 years ago, people began to herd the mouflon in flocks near their villages. The animals then became used to people.

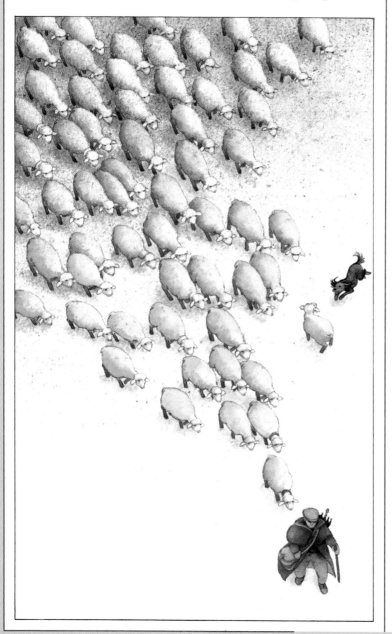

Sheep hate to be alone. They need to live in a flock. Their instinct tells them to stay together, and they follow the leader anywhere—even into danger.

A large flock is not easy to manage. The shepherd's greatest helper is a dog. Sheepdogs learn to round up the sheep and separate one from the flock.

There are more than 800 different breeds of domesticated sheep. Mutton-type sheep have been bred for the meat market; others, like the Merino that live in Australia and the western United States, are bred mainly for their fine wool. Some ewes are kept for their milk, which is used for making cheese and yogurt.

An ewe, lamb, and ram

Goats will eat anything!

When a sheep is alert, it stands still and pricks up its ears. When it's frightened, it scampers away with ears laid back flat.

Sheep are easily startled. When moving in a flock, sheep press closely against one another, often following the oldest ewe. When they graze, the animals face the same direction with their backs to the wind.

A sheep's hooves never stop growing, and must be trimmed if they are not worn down by rough ground. If they aren't trimmed, the animal will start hobbling.

Goats can survive in the poorest of pastures. They know how to find the scarcest blades of grass among dry scrub and rocks. Given the chance, they will eat anything, and will even climb trees to nibble at tender young leaves and shoots.

Goats hate to be penned in. They need to be securely fenced, as they can jump up to nearly five feet (1.5 m) high.

Have a glass of goat's milk! Goats' milk is as nutritious as cows' milk, and is used often in making cheeses. Several million goats are raised in the United States for their meat, milk, skins (for leather), and pelts (for rugs). Cashmere wool comes from goats.

Wild goats and sheep

Wild goats roam the mountains of Asia and India. Wild bighorn sheep live in rugged areas of the western United States.

Cattle have always been important to humans.

The cows you see in the fields seem peaceful enough, but their ancestors, the aurochs, were wild animals indeed. About 6,000 years ago, people began to tame the aurochs.

For the people of ancient civilizations, the bull was often a symbol of strength and power. In ancient Egypt, the sacred bull Apis was worshipped as a god. The Greeks and Cretans often painted pictures of their gods riding on the back of a bull.

Cows are usually kept for their milk; these are dairy cows. Some cows are used for meat as well, but beef cattle tend to be steers.

The Swiss decorate their cattle with flowers to celebrate their return to the valleys after a long summer in the mountains.

Cows are mammals.

Like a human baby, a calf grows inside its mother for nine months. Shortly before the birth, the cow's udder fills with milk to feed her calf. Cows usually have one calf a year, for five or six years. They eat a lot of grass, but they also eat grain, soybeans, and hay. Cows ruminate, or chew cud, which means they chew their food—that they had swallowed earlier—for a second time. You can tell the age of a cow by how worn her teeth are.

For thousands of years people have used oxen for heavy work.

Oxen work hard. Oxen and steer are bulls that have been castrated, which means they cannot father a calf. A castrated bull is quieter and easier to handle than a breeding bull. While steers are primarily raised for beef, oxen are used to work and to pull heavy loads.

For thousands of years, people have used oxen for heavy work, like plowing and pulling carts. Oxen are trained at about two years old. The farmer teaches them to pull a plow at a steady plod and to be harnessed to a cart. Oxen can work for up to 10 hours a day without stopping. Today in most places, oxen have been replaced by tractors.

The mark of the ranch is burned onto the calf's hide with a hot branding iron.

Cowboys and cowgirls, round 'em up! In the western United States, cattle live almost wild in enormous herds on ranches. Ranchers use horses, Jeeps, four-wheelers, and other vehicles, but horses are still the best for rounding up cattle. If an animal strays, the ranch hands catch it with a lasso.

In Australia, farmers use motorbikes, vans, and even helicopters to keep track of their cattle. The animals roam in vast herds over huge areas of land.

In some parts of southern and eastern Europe, people use oxen to pull their carts.

These oxen in China pull a plow to break up the ground.

In the West Indies, oxen pull the carts that take sugar cane from the fields to the factory.

Each cow knows its place in the herd.

Herds of cattle are highly organized.
Each herd has a leader that has reached her position by bullying the others. The leader is often the oldest and strongest of the cows. Every cow learns to know her place, right down to the weakest and most timid, which has to make way for the others.

Cows communicate by lowing, but they mostly make their feelings known by the way they behave to one another. They seem to form friendships and can recognize each other from a long distance away.

If a new cow arrives in a herd, she is often put in a field nearby to give her time to get to know the other animals.

When two cows meet, they stretch out their necks and sniff at each other's muzzles.

When two bulls confront each other, the meeting may end in a violent fight. They paw the ground with their hooves and rub their foreheads against the dirt before coming together with a clash of horns.

Matadors pit their wits against the strength of bulls.

Bulls bred for the bullring are especially spirited and brave. They have long, sharp horns that point forward. A corrida is a battle between a bullfighter, or matador, and a bull. Bullfighting, the national sport of Spain, is also popular in Mexico and Latin America.

"Ride 'em, cowboys and cowgirls!" In rodeos in North America, cowboys and cowgirls try to ride a wild bull or horse, holding on with only one hand. They also compete in calf-roping, bronco-riding, and steer wrestling. In steer wrestling, a rider slides from the horse, grasps the steer's horns, and wrestles it to the ground.

Wild cattle still live in some parts of the world.

Zebu

Zebu have been domesticated for more than 5,000 years. They live in the hot countries of Africa and Asia. The humps on their backs do not contain any bone. They are made only of fat and muscle, providing a store of food for the zebu when times are hard. Some zebu have horns more than three feet (90 cm) long.

Masai boys sometimes must herd their cattle long distances to find grazing and water.

Kuri

The Masai people of East Africa measure their wealth in cattle. The people raise kuri, whose huge horns are hollow, and burn dried cow dung as fuel.

African buffalo

African buffalo live wild on the plains and are dangerous when wounded or scared. Their enemies are lions and people.

Yaks live in the high mountains of Asia. These huge animals can weigh 1,000 pounds (454 kg). Their long coats protect them from the cold temperatures. Yaks give the Tibetans all they need to live: milk, meat, leather, and fur. Wild yaks are now an endangered species.

African buffalo love to wallow in the mud.

Cows are sacred in some countries.

The gaur

The banteng

In India, cows are sacred. They walk through the streets wherever they want to go, and no one will hurt them or eat them. There are even special hospitals for them if they get ill, and some religious temples keep sacred bulls.

In the forests of India, Myanmar, and Nepal lives the fierce gaur. Gaur can be very dangerous, as they are as big as bison and will charge if provoked.

Asian buffalo are called water buffalo, because they love plunging up to their necks in water. Their gentle nature makes them easy to train. They work in the wet paddy fields where rice is grown.

The musk ox of North America has a thick coat to protect it from the bitter weather where it lives.

Musk ox

Bison, a member of the buffalo family

Six million bison once roamed the plains of North America. The Plains Indians depended on them for their meat, fat, skin, and fur. As settlers moved west, they slaughtered most of the bison. Today, you can see small herds of wild buffalo only in national parks and wildlife refuges.

In summer, male bison fight for the right to mate with the females.

In prehistoric times, horses were very small.

The prehistoric ancestor of the horse, the Eohippus, had four toes on each foot and was as small as a fox! Over 60 million years, Eohippus evolved, first to the size of a sheep, then a pony. Soon it had only one toe, which turned into a hoof. Its teeth grew stronger, and it began to eat grass. Prehistoric people first hunted horses for their meat, but then began to capture and tame them to ride.

Wild horses roamed in herds across the steppes of Central Asia. People tried to catch them with lassos.

The first horse riders were the nomads of Central Asia, who began riding in about 3,000 B.C. They were skillful riders, and with no saddles or bridles, they steered the horses with their legs.

Around 400 B.C., the Scythians invented the saddle, a leather frame padded with horsehair and held on by straps called girths. Stirrups, to rest your feet in as you rode, were probably invented by the Chinese in about the fifth century.

The Mongols lived on horseback. They fought, ate, and even slept mounted on their hardy little horses. They ate horse meat and drank milk from the mares. Mongol soldiers usually had five horses each, while officers could have up to 18.

Attila, leader of the Huns, boasted: "Where my horse has passed, the grass will never grow again."

The last wild horses

Przewalski's horses

Przewalski's horse, the only true wild horse, is now extinct in the wild. Hunters in the early 20th century killed off the animal, although a few are left in captivity. Wild horses today are domesticated animals that have been allowed to run free. Their instincts made them revert back to being wild.

Wild herds of Chincoteague ponies live on an island near the state of Maryland.

Forty-one different breeds of horses have originated in the United States.

Wild horses in the United States

About 45,000 wild horses live in the West, especially in Nevada and Montana. The government has been protecting them from domestication since 1971. A stallion leads a herd of wild horses. The stallion fiercely defends his mares and their foals from the advances of other males. If two stallions meet face to face, they will fight. They rear up, lashing out with their hooves and biting each other. The victor wins the right to lead the herd.

Wild stallions fighting

This boy is about to put a halter around his pony's head.

A horse's body is built for speed.

This horse is trotting. Its hooves touch the ground in pairs, the left front with the right back, and vice versa.

Take a look at this horse. Powerful muscles ripple beneath a shining coat. A tough covering, the hoof, protects each foot. A horse has sharp eyes and a sensitive nose. Its ears can hear the slightest sound.

A male horse is called a stallion. Male horses that have been castrated to prevent them from fathering foals are called geldings. A female horse is called a mare. Stallions and geldings have 40 teeth, while mares have 36. You can tell a horse's age by examining how worn its teeth are. Horses' coats come in many different colors, each with a special name, like chestnut, dun, piebald, bay, or dapple gray. A "blaze" is a white streak down a horse's face, and white feet are known as "socks."

A foal is soon standing up and trotting.

The stallion on the left has scented a mare.

The one on the right is neighing.

In the meadow, horses doze in the shade of the trees, swishing their long tails to flick away flies. One of them keeps watch. Horses lie down only if they feel absolutely safe. Usually they rest standing up.

Horses spend more than half the day eating. But unlike cows, horses aren't ruminants; they have only one stomach. They eat grass, hay, oats, bran, barley, and carrots. To tear off the grass, they twist it with their top lip, wedge it between their teeth and pull. Horses drink about eight gallons (30 l) of water each day, and need blocks of salt to lick (salt licks). They love bread and sugar.

Most foals are born in the spring. After 11 months of pregnancy, the mare gives birth. At first, a newborn foal wobbles about on its long legs.

Watch out! A mare will probably kick you if you stand too close to her foal.

A few hours later, the foal will be trotting. Like all mammals, the foal sucks milk from its mother. It can drink up to two and a half gallons (10 l) a day. When it tries to graze, it has to splay out its front legs, because its neck is too short to reach the grass. Foals are curious about everything, but they're very timid too; they rush back to their mothers at the slightest sign of danger.

Working horses

In Mediterranean lands, pack horses carry goods to market in big baskets called panniers, which hang beside the saddle.

Cart horses are extremely strong. Some can pull a load three times their own weight. As they sometimes weigh 2,200 pounds (1,000 kg), that's quite a lot! Years ago, the streets were full of heavy carts being pulled by horses.

Cousins of the horse

Donkeys, mules, and hinnies are also used as pack animals, especially in harsh climates.

Mule

Hinny

Donkey

Sometimes trainers use a long rein, called a lunge, to control a horse. They use the lunge to teach the horse how to jump.

Training starts early, when the young foal learns to walk beside its trainer and obey simple commands. Then it has to get used to wearing a saddle and bridle. By about three years old, it is strong enough to be ridden. Gradually, it learns to respond to its rider and is given more difficult exercises. This process is called "breaking in."

A horse should be groomed daily: its coat brushed to remove dust and mud, and its mane and tail combed. A hoofpick makes sure no stones are stuck under the shoes.

Iron shoes protect a horse's hooves. First, farriers trim the hoof. Then they heat up the shoe so it can be shaped to fit exactly, and they fix it on with eight nails.

1. Mane comb
2. Body brush
3. Metal currycomb
4. Rubber currycomb

Many different sports involve horses.

A game of kabachi

Riding and racing

For centuries, people have used different kinds of horses in a variety challenging sports, from field games such as polo to rodeo and racing.

Polo ponies are fast and agile. The riders change horses several times during the game.

In harness racing, the horses are not allowed to gallop. They are trained to trot very fast, pulling a small cart called a "sulky."

Horses and sports

The Russian sport of kabachi is also played in Argentina. The rider tries to hurl a stick through a ring mounted on a long pole.

In polo, two teams of four riders hit a wooden ball with mallets. Polo ponies have to be fast, strong, and well-trained.

The thoroughbred is the fastest horse. All the best racehorses are thoroughbreds, born and raised on stud farms. In the United States, thoroughbreds are registered with the American Jockey Club. Each horse is given an official name and a number is tattooed inside its lip. The riders compete in two main types of horse races: a flat race, like the Kentucky Derby, and a steeplechase, like the Grand National, where horses jump fences as they gallop around the track.

Flat racing

Intriguing facts, activities, games, a quiz, and a glossary, followed by the index

■ Classifying animals

Because so many different species of animals exist, scientists have arranged them into groups based on their individual characteristics.

The right-hand column lists some of the major groups, such as fish or birds. Not all animal groups are shown here. Choose an animal shown, such as a hamster.

Find out in which group it belongs, using the diagram.

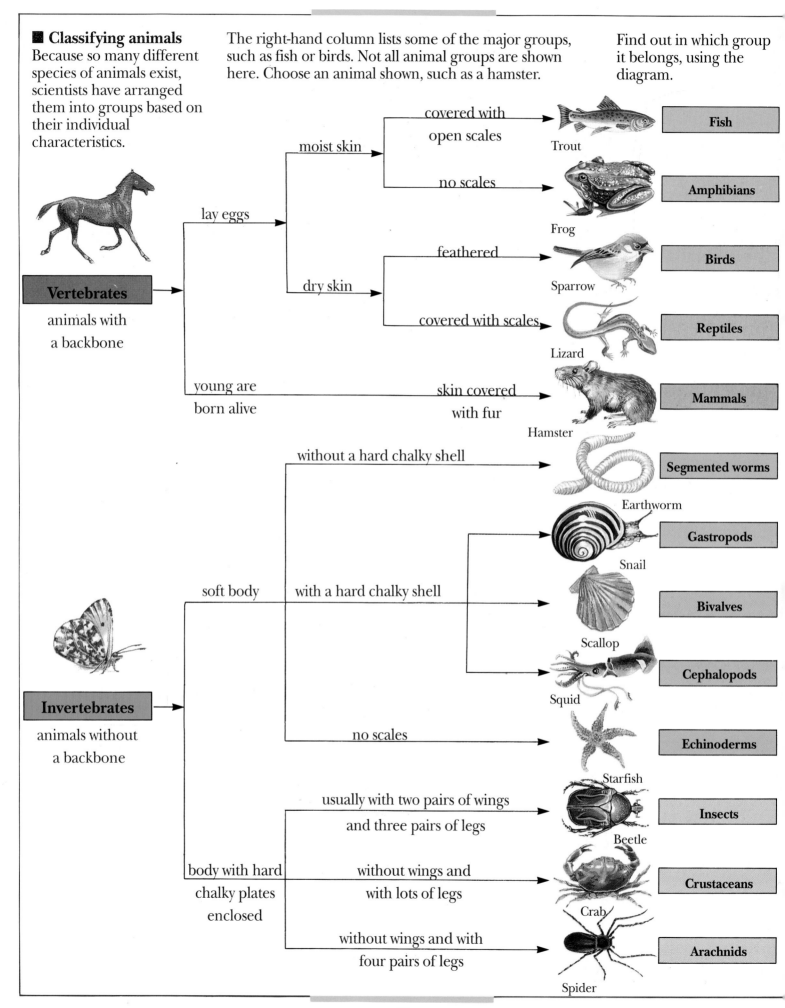

Vertebrates
animals with a backbone

lay eggs

moist skin

covered with open scales → Trout → **Fish**

no scales → Frog → **Amphibians**

dry skin

feathered → Sparrow → **Birds**

covered with scales → Lizard → **Reptiles**

young are born alive

skin covered with fur → Hamster → **Mammals**

Invertebrates
animals without a backbone

soft body

without a hard chalky shell → Earthworm → **Segmented worms**

with a hard chalky shell → Snail → **Gastropods**

→ Scallop → **Bivalves**

→ Squid → **Cephalopods**

no scales → Starfish → **Echinoderms**

body with hard chalky plates enclosed

usually with two pairs of wings and three pairs of legs → Beetle → **Insects**

without wings and with lots of legs → Crab → **Crustaceans**

without wings and with four pairs of legs → Spider → **Arachnids**

■ Did you know?

Some people have unusual pets! They keep chameleons, lizards, or snakes in a terrarium. Chameleons come from Africa and Asia. They shoot out a long tongue with a sticky tip to catch the insects they eat.

The royal python is not as big as other pythons. It is a sluggish, docile snake that does well in captivity. It swallows a mouse whole every day.

Some tortoises are protected. Desert tortoises are protected by the U.S. Department of Fish and Wildlife Service. They live in deserts and open woods of the Southwest. A desert tortoise can be more than a foot (30 cm) long as a full-grown adult.

Tortoises live for a long time. Some have even reached 150 years of age! Decorations on vases and murals show us that even in ancient times, people living around the Mediterranean used to keep tortoises as pets. People also played a musical instrument with strings pulled taut across a hollow tortoise shell.

Barn swallows stick their nests onto vertical walls and under ledges. The nests are cup-shaped and made from a mixture of mud, sand, clay, straw, hair from cattle and horses, fine roots, blades of grass, and feathers.

Swallows often nest in colonies and usually come back to the same nest every year to lay their eggs. They take great trouble repairing any damage that has occurred during their winter away.

The oldest swallows' nest documented was 48 years old and must have been used as a home for 200 to 300 chicks. In human terms, that would mean generations of children stretching over more than 1,000 years!

Have you ever found a cowbird's nest? No, because cowbirds don't build a nest, nor do they bring up their own young.

The female cowbird looks for the nest of a small, insect-eating bird, a sparrow for instance. She watches carefully until the owners are away, and then secretly lays her egg in it. She lays a single egg in several nests, choosing those where the eggs look most like hers.

Unknowingly, the hosts sit on the egg along with their own. The cowbird chick hatches earlier than the others, and as soon as it is out of its shell, it pushes the other eggs over the edge of the nest.

Being the only mouth to feed, the chick grows rapidly and is soon as big as its foster parents. They continue to feed it for six weeks, until it is ready to fly, even if it has grown too big for the nest!

Watch out for fleas! Fleas don't hang around. They just stay long enough on the back of an animal to suck a meal of blood!

Then they fall to the ground. Each one lays several hundred eggs, which hatch into hairy grubs, rather like small caterpillars. A month later, the grubs have turned into pupae and lie waiting in their cocoons. As soon as another animal walks nearby, the vibration in the floor stimulates the adult fleas to hatch, and they hop onto the unfortunate animal. Fleas are so hungry, it sometimes takes several bites to satisfy their appetites!

Why should you never cut a cat's whiskers? Whiskers act as feelers, sensitive to currents of air or obstacles in the cat's path. They are almost like a radar system, helping the cat find its way in the dark.

Why do pigs have such a bad reputation? Probably because they enjoy rolling in the mud, people came to think of them as dirty animals. The Greek historian Herodotus wrote about the ancient Egyptians: "If a man passing accidentally touches a pig, he instantly hurries to the river and plunges in with all his clothes on!"

A swineherd did not have the right to go into the temple, and he could only marry the daughter of another swineherd.

Even today, eating meat from pigs is forbidden to religious Jews and Muslims.

More than 10,000 years ago, prehistoric people began domesticating wild dogs.

The Egyptians used to take their cats with them when they went hunting along the banks of the Nile.

Roman women enjoyed keeping tame squirrels as pets. They would carry them around on their shoulders.

Why do cats eat grass? Grass helps food pass through the digestive system and allows the cat to bring up balls of the fur it swallowed when it licked itself clean.

Where do goldfish come from? Related to carp, goldfish come from China, where they have been raised for 1,000 years. They were carefully bred from a fish that was grayish-green. Goldfish arrived in Europe in the 18th century, when the East India Company produced some at the court of King Louis XV of France. They soon became very popular.

Hungry mouths! Once goldfish have laid and fertilized their eggs, you must remove the parent fish from the aquarium, otherwise they will eat their young! The female lays between 500 and 1,000 eggs, each about the size of a grain of tapioca.

■ Did you know?

Wild cattle still live on the island of Bali.
For thousands of years, people living on the Indonesian island of Bali have been domesticating bantengs, the wild cattle that live in the local forests. The animals provide meat for food and are trained to work in the fields.

Banteng

The world's fastest cows are Maduran cattle,
a cross between a banteng and a zebu. These animals can gallop as fast as a horse, up to 43 miles (70 km) per hour.

Every year on the island of Madura in Indonesia, the people organize cattle races. The cows are harnessed together in pairs, and the crowd places bets for the winners. It's an exciting event for everyone.

Zebu

Honey bees dance! When a honey bee discovers a new source of nectar, she returns to the hive and dances for the other bees. If she dances in a circle, the nectar source is within 100 yards (91 m). If the source is farther away, the bee will perform a waggle dance. The other bees know exactly where to find the nectar source by the type of dance and by matching the scent of nectar on the flower with the scent on her body.

Why do we keep our money in piggy banks? In Southeast Asia during the 12th and 13th centuries, owning a pig was a symbol of wealth, and pottery pigs stuffed with money were offered as gifts. By the 17th century, the idea of the piggy bank had spread across Europe, and pigs came to be linked with the idea of payment and money.

The Ancient Greeks believed that a great winged horse called Pegasus carried lightning across the skies.

The unicorn is a mythical horse with a single horn in the middle of its forehead.

The powerful centaurs of Greek mythology are creatures that are half man and half horse.

The world's smallest horse is the Falabella from Argentina, which is about the size of a dog. This animal is usually 34 inches high (86 cm) or smaller. The smallest Falabella in the world is on display at Land of Little Horses in Gettysburg, Pennsylvania. Falabellas are expensive. They can cost anywhere from $1,500 to $100,000, depending upon their size.

Horse power
At a walk, a horse can pull a load many times as heavy as itself: an animal weighing 880 pounds (400 kg) can pull something that weighs 4,400 pounds (2,000 kg) along a flat road at about two miles (3.5 km) per hour.

Raccoons have good table manners! They wash their food before they eat it. They like living in the suburbs, rummaging in the garbage cans for food.

■ Quiz

Can you answer these questions? The correct answers are at the bottom of the page.

1. How many calves does a cow have per year?
a. one
b. four
c. six

2. Which teeth does a pig use to fight (a farmer clips them so piglets don't hurt each other)?
a. incisors
b. molars
c. canines

3. How many toes does a pig have on each foot?
a. two
b. four
c. five

4. How many legs do insects have?
a. two
b. six
c. eight

5. A rabbit's home is called a
a. nest.
b. mound.
c. hutch.

6. How can you tell the age of a horse?
a. look at its eyes
b. look at its tail
c. look at its teeth

7. How long does a mare carry her foal before it is born?
a. six months
b. 11 months
c. 365 days

8. Which is the tallest dog in the world?
a. German shepherd
b. Irish wolfhound
c. Saint Bernard

9. Which is the smallest dog in the world?
a. Chihuahua
b. Basset hound
c. Yorkshire terrier

10. How much weight can an ant lift?
a. 50 times its body weight
b. three times its body weight
c. its own body weight

11. How many kittens can a cat have in a litter?
a. less than four
b. up to six
c. nine to 12

12. Pigs roll in mud
a. to get dirty.
b. to get warm.
c. to keep cool.

13. Which of these animals does not hibernate?
a. tortoise
b. bear
c. pigeon

14. Bats make sounds that humans can't hear because they are
a. too low.
b. too high.
c. silent (bats don't make a sound).

15. Which of these animals does not lay eggs?
a. garden spider
b. snail
c. mouse

16. How long does it take for ducks to hatch?
a. 28 days
b. 28 hours
c. 28 weeks

■ How can you attract more birds to your yard?

Put up a bird feeder.
Make sure you keep it full all year long because the birds will become dependent on it for food.

Make a bird bath. But don't put it near a cat! It will hide and pounce on the birds.

Plant flowers, like columbine, to attract hummingbirds.

Hedgehogs make special pets!
African pygmy hedgehogs are becoming popular pets in the United States and Canada. These small hedgehogs fit in your hands and are quiet, shy, and easy to care for.

■ True or false?

Are these statements true or false?
Check your answer at the bottom of the right-hand column.

1. Ants are enemies of termites.

2. If you are stung by a bee, you should rub the spot.

3. A bee can fly at 15.5 miles (25 km) per hour.

A wasp

4. Wasps are bigger than bees.

5. Ants are pests and do little good.

6. A large nest of ants can eat 10,000 insects a day.

7. Ants sting.

8. Soldier termites squirt poison at their enemies.

9. A hornet is at least twice as big as a wasp.

10. Garden spiders can be dangerous.

A soldier termite defends its mound against ants.

■ Take a closer look at the animals around you.

Ants are amazing workers.
To observe them, find an anthill in the cracks of a sidewalk or in your lawn. Sprinkle some sugared bread crumbs near the anthill. Watch the ants try to carry the crumbs back to the nest.

Bats! A single brown bat can eat 3,000 to 7,000 mosquitoes in one night! They are good to have close by. Buy a bat house and hang it at least 10 feet (3 m) above the ground. It should be placed where there is lots of sun and near a source of water. A bat can live for 20 years.

If you find a bird with a ring around its leg,
contact the U.S. Fish and

Wildlife Service. Tell them about the markings on the ring, what kind of bird it was, and the date and place you found it. Ringing birds helps scientists understand the habits and migratory patterns of different species.

Answers: 1. True, 2. False (you'll rub the sting in if you do), 3. True, 4. False, 5. False (they help air get to plant roots), 6. True, 7. True (but only some kinds), 8. True (glands spray poison from their foreheads), 9. True, 10. False (unless you're a fly! Garden spiders don't sting)

■ Did you know?

Wolves communicate using visual signals. Their bodies show how they feel. Dogs and wolves are alike: you can tell a dog's mood just by watching its behavior.

Normal

Threatening

Submissive

On the alert

Dominant

Completely submissive

Coats of many colors

Horses' coats come in lots of different colors, each with a special name. Some colors are obvious, like brown or chestnut. Others can keep you guessing. Horses with white coats are known as "grays," and a horse is only truly black if its muzzle is black as well. Piebald is a white coat with black patches, and skewbald is a white coat with patches of brown or any other color.

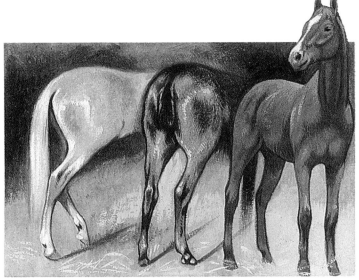

Grey   Brown   Bay

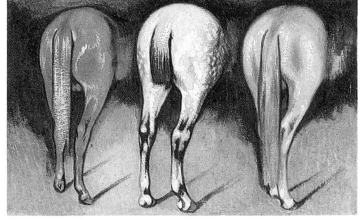

Chestnut   Dapple gray   Palomino

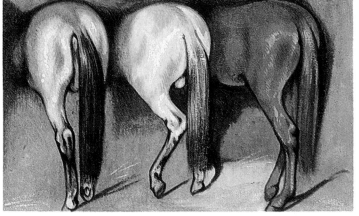

Roan   Dun   Liver chestnut

It's fun to learn to recognize birds. Look at the shape of their beak or their wings as they fly, and make a note of their habits. Listen to their song. These are all clues to help you identify birds.

House martin

Swallow

Swift

Barn owls leave their traces around town. At the foot of a tree or in a barn, you may find the pellets they regurgitate after eating a mouse or a little bird.

The pellets contain the bones, feathers, skin—and everything else the owl can't digest. The pellets can tell you what the owl ate that night.

■ Did you know?

Learn to recognize animals from their prints.

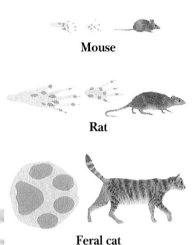

Mouse

Rat

Feral cat
(domestic cat gone wild)

What about keeping fish in an aquarium?
Goldfish can live for 15 years if you look after them well. Or you might prefer saltwater tropical fish with their stunning colors.

An aquarium, in which the water is filtered and oxygenated, is better than an ordinary bowl. Regulate the temperature and use fresh or salt water, depending on the type of fish you are keeping.

■ How many different butterflies are shown below?
Does it look like 10? Actually, there are only five. Each one is shown with its wings folded, and then farther down with wings spread. Can you match up the pairs?

Solutions to the butterfly game:
1 and d = Orange tip
2 and a = Purple Emperor
5 and c = Heliconius antiochus
3 and b = Comma
4 and e = Grayling

It's exciting to see an animal in the wild!
If you live near a forest or out in the country near farmlands, take a friend with you and search for a fox's den. Foxes usually build their den in an enlarged groundhog hole. At the entrance to the hole, the dirt may be stained with blackberry juice and strewn with feathers, fur, and bones. Don't touch anything, or the fox won't come back. Hide a couple of yards away, facing the wind, so your scent is carried away. Then be silent and patient. The fox may reappear.

69

■ Glossary

Bird of prey: a large bird, such as an eagle, falcon or owl, which kills smaller birds or mammals for food. It has sharp talons (claws) and a strong beak.

Camouflage: a way of hiding by blending in with the surroundings. Many wild animals have skin, fur, or shells that match the backgrounds in which they live. This makes it easier to hunt and avoid predators.

Chrysalis: the form a caterpillar takes before turning into a butterfly or moth.

Cocoon: the silky case spun by some larvae to protect them in the chrysalis stage.

Crustacean: one of the largest groups of animals. They have a hard outer shell. Most (such as crabs, lobsters, and shrimps) live in water, but the woodlouse —which lives on land— is also a member of this animal group.

Ecosystem: a community of different species interacting with one another and the non-living elements of the environment.

Hibernate: to spend the winter months in a deep sleep. Many small animals such as pocket mice and woodchucks hibernate.

Hinny: offspring of a male horse and a female donkey that have mated.

Larva: an insect in the first stage of its life, after it comes out of its egg.

Litter: a group of young animals born to one mother at the same time.

Mammals: the group of animals in which the mothers nurse their young with milk; most bear their young live.

Mandible: the jaw of an insect or crustacean.

Insects have a pair of upper jaws, rather than an upper and lower jaw, as a dog has.

Membrane: a thin skin or covering.

Migrate: when an animal or bird moves according to the season, often to find new pastures or warmer climates.

70

Mongols: in the 13th century, Genghis Khan led this army to conquer China, and then went on to invade Europe.

Mule: offspring of a male donkey and a female horse with the size of a horse and the appearance of a donkey.

Mummy: body of a human being or an animal embalmed for burial, as was the custom in Ancient Egypt.

Nomads: people who do not settle but roam from place to place looking for fresh pasture for their herds.

Oxygen: a colorless, odorless gas found in the air we breathe.

Pollen: a fine, yellow powder found in flowers and used in the

reproduction of plants.

Pollinate: to move pollen from one flower to another, often done by a flying insect, resulting in the fertilization of plants.

Pupa: a chrysalis; the non-feeding, largely immobile stage in some insect life cycles.

Pupil: black, circular opening in the center of the eye that lets in light. In daylight, a cat's pupils close down to narrow slits.

Rodent: small mammal with incisor teeth that continue to grow as they are worn down.

Ruminant: any kind of animal that chews cud, like cows and deer.

Saliva: fluid some animals produce in the mouth to help them swallow and digest food more easily.

Secrete: to produce a substance in the body, like saliva in the mouth.

Species: a group of animals whose members are related and can breed with each other.

Spinnerets: a spider's tiny organ that spins silk for its cocoons and webs. The silk starts as a sticky liquid which hardens in the air to form a light, strong thread.

Steer: a bull that has been castrated, which means it cannot father a calf. Steers are raised for beef, a food.

Terrarium: a special container or enclosure, set up with the right conditions for keeping reptiles or plants.

■ Have you heard these expressions?

"You have ants in your pants."
You are very fidgety.

"He has bats in the belfry."
He's full of crazy ideas.

"You've got a bee in your bonnet."
You are obsessed with a particular idea.

"As the crow flies"
Distance measured in a straight line

"The chicken has flown the coop."
A person got away.

"Birds of a feather flock together."
People who are alike tend to group together.

"To kill two birds with one stone"
To achieve two goals with a single action

"A bird's-eye view"
A clear view from high up

"I have butterflies in my stomach."
I have a nervous feeling in my stomach.

"A bull in a china shop"
An insensitive person in a delicate situation

"That's like red rag to a bull."
Something that is bound to make a person angry

"To take the bull by the horns"
To try to find a solution to a problem without hesitating

"You're the cat's meow."
You're very fine.

"Curiosity killed the cat."
Trying to find out too much about other people's business can lead to disaster.

"To set the cat among the pigeons"
To stir things up; to cause trouble

"When the cat's away, the mice will play."
When the person in charge is not there, people tend to do what they like.

"Don't let the cat out of the bag."
Don't give the secret away by mistake.

"You're like a cat on a hot tin roof."
You're very nervous or excited.

"He looks like something the cat brought in."
He looks a mess.

"Has the cat got your tongue?"
Why are you silent?

"I want to see which way the cat jumps."
I want to wait for the result to show itself.

"Don't count your chickens before they're hatched."
Don't depend too much on something that hasn't happened yet.

"You'll have to wait till the cows come home."
You'll have to wait for a long time.

"To make a dog's dinner of something"
To make a mess of something

"A shaggy dog story"
A long story or joke with a pointless ending

"He was like a dog with two tails."
He was really happy.

"To put the cart before the horse"
To do things in the wrong order

"She heard it straight from the horse's mouth."
She heard it directly from the source.

"Hold your horses."
Stop; wait a moment.

"Donkey's years"
A very long time

"When pigs fly."
That is very unlikely to happen; never

"Don't make a pig of yourself."
Don't eat too much.

"He looks like a drowned rat."
He is a wet, untidy mess.

"A wolf in sheep's clothing"
Someone who appears to be mild and gentle but does in fact have evil intentions

"To cry wolf"
To raise a false alarm